D1135014

A Clue in Code

A Sam and Dave Mystery Story

A CLUE IN CODE

. . . .

Marilyn Singer

illustrated by
Judy Glasser

HARPER & ROW, PUBLISHERS

A Clue in Code
Text copyright © 1985 by Marilyn Singer
Illustrations copyright © 1985 by Judy Glasser
All rights reserved. No part of this book may be
used or reproduced in any manner whatsoever without
written permission except in the case of brief quotations
embodied in critical articles and reviews. Printed in
the United States of America. For information address
Harper & Row Junior Books, 10 East 53rd Street,
New York, N.Y. 10022. Published simultaneously in
Canada by Fitzhenry & Whiteside Limited, Toronto.
Designed by Trish Parcell
10 9 8 7 6 5 4 3 2 1
First Edition

Library of Congress Cataloging in Publication Data
Singer, Marilyn.
   A clue in code.

   Summary: When money for the class trip suddenly
disappears, detective twins Sam and Dave Bean get on the
case.
   1. Children's stories, American. [1. Mystery and
detective stories. 2. Twins—Fiction] I. Glasser, Judy,
ill. II. Title.
PZ7.S6172Cl 1985   [Fic]   84-48335
ISBN 0-06-025634-6
ISBN 0-06-025637-0 (lib. bdg.)

1

The curve ball came at him in slow motion. His bat, tugging at his arms, was poised, ready. He swung, and the swing was clean and smooth. *Crack!* Bat and ball connected. The white sphere soared over the pitcher's head, arced high above the outfield and landed smack in the hands of some lucky fan in the stands. As he crossed home plate, he heard the crowd call his name, "Sam Bean! Sam Bean!"

". . . did you, Sam Bean?"

Sam's eyes focused slowly. The fans, the stands, the field dissolved. The cheers of the crowd turned to giggles. It took him a moment to realize where he was and who was talking to him. When he did, he turned red. "Uh, I'm sorry, Ms. Corfein," Sam said to his teacher. "Could you repeat the question?"

The class giggled again.

"Asleep on the job, eh, Sam?" Ms. Corfein said.

"Way to go, Bean," Willie Landers, sitting next to Sam, snickered. Willie was a tough kid who always made snide remarks—especially to Sam and Dave, Sam's identical twin brother. Willie—and practically everybody else in the school—knew their reputation as private eyes, only unlike most other people, Willie disliked them for it.

"Sorry," Sam mumbled again. It wasn't like him to daydream in school, but the November day was so gloomy, he'd got to thinking about April and baseball and the next thing he knew he'd dozed off. He glanced over at his brother. Dave wasn't looking at him. He was taking some money out of his pocket, and he looked alert as always.

"I asked you if you brought in your money for the class trip. You and Roger Blitzman were the only ones who didn't raise your hands," said Ms. Corfein.

This time, Sam glanced at Roger. He was a small, shy boy whom nobody knew very well. He kept pretty much to himself. Ms. Corfein was always calling on him to do jobs for her. He might have been called "teacher's pet," except he didn't act like one.

"Oh. Oh yeah. I brought it," said Sam.

"Good. Roger, would you please collect the money, put it in this envelope and put the envelope in my locker. Here's the key."

Roger stumbled to his feet and began to walk around the room, collecting the money. Sam turned to look at him just as he was putting the envelope in. Then Roger locked the door and returned the key to Ms. Corfein.

"All right, class. Turn to page forty-one of your workbook," Ms. Corfein said.

The class groaned softly.

"Rita, tell us the answer to problem one." Ms. Corfein shivered slightly, went over to the long row of windows and began to fiddle with one of them.

Sam watched her for a moment, then opened his book. The numbers began to swim in front of his eyes. He had just hit his third homer when the lunch bell rang. Three more hours to go. I can tell nothing is going to happen today. Nothing at all, Sam thought.

In less than an hour, he'd find out just how wrong he was.

2

Dave Bean left the cafeteria early because it was his turn to feed Burble the gerbil. When he got to the classroom, there, in the doorway, was Willie Landers. Dave didn't hang around with Willie. Besides the fact that he was rude and surly, he had a bad reputation. The year before, Willie had stolen stuff from Everett's candy store and from several kids at school and gotten caught. His father, Mr. Landers, the school custodian, had come down hard on him, and Willie hadn't been in serious trouble since. But nobody wanted to tangle with him. "Hi, Willie," Dave said casually.

Willie didn't bother with a greeting. "You're here early," Dave said.

Willie sneered. "What's it to you, cop . . ." But the tough guy effect was ruined by a huge sneeze. Dave waited to see if he was going to wipe his nose on his sleeve, but, instead, Willie groped in his pocket, pulled out a big, wadded handkerchief and shook it out. Something small and metallic bounced onto the floor. Dave stooped to pick it up.

"Leave that alone," Willie said, grabbing for it.

But not before Dave saw that it was a key. Willie pocketed it and walked hurriedly away, blowing his nose.

Dave shook his head and entered the classroom. Patti Terroni, perfectly dressed as usual, was there, scratching Burble.

"Hey, Patti, it's my turn to feed him today," Dave said.

"Is it? Are you sure? I thought it was mine."

"Ms. Corfein keeps the list in this drawer." Dave pulled it out. "See, 11/12—Dave Bean; 11/13—Patti Terroni."

"Uh oh, I guess I blew it. Sorry. . . . But I'm not the only one who's confused. Willie was here when I arrived. He said it was *his* turn to feed Burble."

"Willie? It's not his turn until next week."

"I wasn't going to get into an argument with Willie Landers." Patti smiled, showing off her perfect teeth.

Dave smiled back. The thought crossed his mind that if he were interested in girls, he might be interested in Patti Terroni. But he wasn't interested in girls.

The bell rang. Dave and Patti took their seats and watched the rest of the class dribble in.

They were all seated when Ms. Corfein came in and walked to her locker. Dave watched her open it. A white envelope fluttered to the floor. She picked it up. And then she let out a gasp.

The class jumped.

She turned to them, her face white. She held out the envelope, turned it upside down and shook it. It was empty. "All right. Who took it? Who took the class trip money?"

There was another gasp—this time from the students—and then, a shocked silence as everyone turned to look at each other. Sam looked at Willie, who had a puzzled frown on his face. Dave and Rita O'Toole raised their eyebrows at each other. Patti let out a nervous giggle.

"I said, who did it?"

"Ms. Corfein, it must have happened during lunchtime," Rita said.

"Why?" demanded Ms. Corfein.

"Roger put the money in the locker, right?"

Everyone looked at Roger, who sank a little lower in his seat and nodded.

"Nobody went near that locker after Roger. Then we left for lunch," Rita finished reasonably.

Sam couldn't help but smile a little. Rita was a good friend of his and Dave's ever since they had found her missing brother a couple of months ago. Sam thought she was the smartest kid he'd ever met—next to Dave.

"Hmmm," said Ms. Corfein. "Who fed Burble today?"

"Uh, I did," Patti and Dave said simultaneously. "What?"

Patti explained the mix-up and added that Willie had been there as well.

"Willie was here?" Ms. Corfein looked at him.

"Yeah, I was. So what?" Willie sneered.

"Once a thief, always a thief," muttered Darryl Gaines.

Willie gave him a nasty look. Darryl gave Willie one back. It was no secret that Darryl hated Willie's guts. He was one of the kids Willie had taken money from.

"Ms. Corfein," Rita put in. "The door's always

open. Anyone could get in here during lunch."

"That's true," Ms. Corfein agreed.

"But how did someone open Ms. Corfein's locker?" Dave said and asked permission to look at the lock. "It hasn't been tampered with."

Even though Sam knew that Dave had gotten the expression from a detective movie they'd watched the week before, he felt proud of his brother for using it.

"And only Ms. Corfein has the key to it," Dave finished.

"Only Ms. Corfein and Mr. Landers," added Patti Terroni.

Darryl spoke, "Like I said, once a thief . . ."

This time everyone looked at Willie. And it seemed to Sam that he was upset.

3

By the end of the day, the whole school was buzzing with the news about the stolen money. Mr. Bryant announced over the loudspeaker that the person who removed some "items" from Ms. Corfein's locker was to return them immediately, and "no questions would be asked," but so far, no one had returned the money.

Just as the last bell rang, a reporter from *The Dart*, the school newspaper, came to interview Ms. Corfein and some of the kids. Ms. Corfein picked Dave, Rita and several other students as interviewees. Sam didn't want to be interviewed. He wanted to go to the lockers and hear what some of the other kids were saying about the robbery. "Want me to get your stuff and meet you back here?" he asked Dave and Rita.

"Thanks, Sam," Dave said. "You know my combination."

"Yes, thanks," said Rita. "Here's mine." She quickly wrote down the numbers on a scrap of paper.

Sam went to his locker first and took out his jacket. He was eager to talk to Dave and Rita about the day's events. He closed his locker and opened Dave's.

Patti Terroni and Darryl Gaines appeared. "You think Willie did it?" Patti asked.

"Who else?" said Darryl. "That creep's the only one who would've done it."

"You don't think there are any other crooks around this school?" Patti kidded him.

Darryl was about to answer when Willie sauntered in. Something was funny about the way he was holding his hand against his shirt. It's like he's hiding something, thought Sam.

Patti and Darryl looked at Willie. "This school used to be high class," Darryl said. He and Patti walked away.

Acting as if he weren't staring, Sam watched Willie out of the corner of his eye. Willie twirled at his lock. It seemed to be sticking. He punched at it. Finally, the lock clicked open. From under his shirt, Willie took out a brown, rectangular envelope. He put it in his locker. Then he took out his jacket, slammed the locker and sauntered away.

Darryl ran back in. "Forgot my hat," he muttered, opening his locker again, taking out a cap and jamming it on top of his short Afro.

I wonder what was in that envelope, thought Sam. He moved on to Rita's locker. He had to keep looking from the scrap of paper in his hand to the lock's dial.

Roger Blitzman and some other kids arrived. One said, "I hear they're searching everyone at the door. You can't leave until you've been searched."

"Yeah?" said another.

Bang! The sharp sound made Sam jump. He whirled around. Roger Blitzman's books had fallen out of his open locker.

Sam looked at the pile of books at Roger's feet. "Looks like you need a shopping cart," Sam joked. "Here, I'll help you." He put the coats in Rita's locker and started picking up the books. "You like to read whodunnits, huh?" Sam said, noticing the large proportion of mysteries.

Roger nodded. His shyness made Sam bolder than he usually was with people.

"Well, if you come across one that tells you who stole the class money, let me know, okay?"

Roger brushed his hand across his forehead. "Heh-heh," he laughed nervously.

"Well, 'bye," said Sam, gathering up the coats from Rita's locker. Poor guy, he thought, he's even shyer than I am. Then Sam went to meet Dave and Rita.

4

"I still say it could've been anyone," Rita said as she, Dave and Sam stood waiting for Rita's mother to pick her up. Usually, she took the bus, but on Tuesdays she had piano lessons which her mother drove her to.

"Maybe, but Patti and Willie were both there when I went to feed Burble. Willie was hanging around outside acting funny," Dave said. "He dropped a key and got really upset when I tried to pick it up for him."

"You didn't tell me that! What kind of key?" Rita

asked. "Could it have been a key to a locker?"

"Maybe, but I don't know. I keep thinking it was bigger than a locker key. I'm not sure, though. I don't know what Ms. Corfein's key looks like. I suppose I could ask to see it, but I don't think I'd remember if Willie's was the same key."

He turned to Sam, who had been quiet through most of the discussion.

"I saw Willie put a big, brown envelope into his locker," Sam said slowly.

"What was in it?"

"I don't know."

"Then it's got to be Willie who's the thief," Rita said.

"I don't know," said Sam, even more slowly.

"What do you mean? He was in the classroom at lunchtime. He had access to making a copy of Ms. Corfein's key . . ." Rita paused.

Sam didn't want to ask her what *access* meant. He liked to try to figure out Rita's thousand-dollar words without asking, and besides, he didn't want to seem dumb.

"And he even had a key he didn't want Dave to know about. He was seen by Sam putting a big, brown envelope in his locker. Furthermore, he has a record of stealing," Rita finished. "It's got to be Willie."

"I don't know," Sam insisted.

14

"What is it, Sam?" Dave asked, looking seriously at his brother. "What's bugging you?"

"It's just . . . when Ms. Corfein yelled that the money had been stolen, I looked at Willie and he . . . he didn't look guilty. He looked confused, but not guilty. And definitely not happy."

"So, maybe he's a good actor," Rita said.

"No," said Sam, firmly this time. "He's a terrible actor."

"Sam's right," Dave agreed. "When he got caught stealing last year, he tried to lie, and he turned bright red and blew the whole thing."

"So what are you guys going to do?"

"I think we should go over to Willie's and talk to him. What do you think, Sam?"

Sam nodded.

"I wish I could come too, but here's my mom," said Rita.

Sam was sorry to see her go. He always liked her company, even though he still felt a little shy around her. He waved at her and Ms. O'Toole and, with Dave, headed for Willie's house.

On the way there, at the playground they passed every day, they saw Patti Terroni and a girl named Mona Green, who was in Mr. Tomas's class. Patti and Mona were sitting on a stone turtle, looking at something. They were so engrossed they didn't see Sam or Dave.

"This one's worth a lot, Patti," Mona was saying. "A buyer might pay twenty-five dollars for it."

"Twenty-five dollars! That is a lot," Patti said.

"Hi, Patti. Hello, Mona," Dave called. "What's worth twenty-five dollars?"

Patti looked up and flashed a big smile. "Oh hi, Dave. This old movie magazine that was my mother's. . . . So, are you and Sam going to investigate the robbery?"

"Maybe."

"Well, you probably won't have much to investigate. Everybody knows Willie did it."

Dave didn't reply. "See you tomorrow, Patti," he said.

"See you," she answered and went back to looking at her magazine.

"I think she likes you," Sam teased when they were out of Patti's earshot.

"I think so too," Dave said confidently.

Sam sighed. Sometimes Dave's confidence was a bit overwhelming.

They reached Willie's house and rang the bell once, twice, three times. No one answered.

"What do we do now?" Sam asked.

"Come back after supper."

"Do *you* think Willie did it?"

Dave sighed. "I don't know. He really does seem the most likely suspect, though."

"Yeah. But you know what they say in mystery stories."

"What?"

"That it's never the most likely suspect who did it."

"Maybe that's true for mystery stories," Dave replied, "but it's not true for real life."

"Hmmmm," said Sam.

5

The street was dark and quiet. The midautumn chill made Sam and Dave pull their coat collars higher. They had just reached the Landers' house. The blue light of a TV shone through the front window.

"Well, somebody's home this time," Dave said.

"*Shh.* Look," Sam whispered.

Dave turned his head. A short, stocky figure was slipping out of a second-story window and sliding down a drainpipe.

"Willie! Let's trail him," Dave said.

He and Sam stood in the shadows until Willie was far enough ahead of them. Then they followed him. He didn't look back at all, just walked swiftly, head down, as if he knew exactly where he was going. He turned the corner, strode down Apple Street, crossed over and turned down Pear Place.

"He's heading for our school," Sam murmured. His toe hit a can. It clattered into the gutter.

"Get back," Dave said again. They stepped behind a bush.

Just in time, because Willie turned his head and stared right at the spot where they'd been standing. Then he shrugged and walked on. In a few minutes, he reached the school. He walked around to the rear.

"There are no bushes; we'll have to hug the building and hope he doesn't spot us," Dave whispered. Then he said, *"Wow!"*

"I can't see. What's he doing?" asked Sam.

"He's letting himself in through the fire exit."

"He's breaking in?"

"No, I think he's got a key."

Click. The door closed behind Willie. "Okay, let's go," Dave said. He and Sam scooted to the door. "Locked," Dave said. "Now how do we get in?"

"I think I know a way," said Sam. "Follow me." He led Dave around the building. He carefully surveyed the wall. "Now, which one is it? This one, I think." He climbed up onto a windowsill. He was right below Ms. Corfein's classroom, which was on the second floor.

"Sam, what are you doing?"

He didn't answer, just stepped up on the hinges of the window and stretched as high as he could. He reached the ledge of the window directly above. Straining, he began to pull himself up.

"Be careful," Dave warned.

Sam grunted and got first one knee, then the other, on the ledge.

"What *are* you doing, Sam?"

Sam pushed on the glass. "If I'm right, this is the one Ms. Corfein couldn't close . . . ahhh." The window swung open just wide enough for a skinny kid to squeeze through. "Come on," Sam called, easing himself inside.

"Couldn't you have found an easier way?" Dave groaned and began to climb up, huffing and puffing the whole way.

"Good work." Sam grinned as Dave made it through the window.

Dave blew him a raspberry.

"Now, where do you think he went?" Sam asked.

"From what you told me before, I have an idea. But we better hurry up. He may not stick around long. This time, you follow me." He opened the classroom door. "Be very, very quiet."

"It's dark in here," Sam whispered, taking out the flashlight he always carried as part of his detective kit.

"No lights until I say 'Now,' " Dave said.

"Okay."

They left the room and groped their way down the corridor. When they rounded the corner, they saw a faint light at the far end and heard scrabbling sounds.

Hardly daring to breathe, they tiptoed down the hall, nearer and nearer to the light.

Suddenly, Dave hollered, "Now!" and he and Sam both turned on their flashlights.

There, in front of his open locker, with a flashlight propped in the door, was Willie Landers. In one hand he held a big, brown envelope; in the other, a wad of money.

"Okay, Willie," Dave said. "We caught you red-hand—"

The look on Willie's face stopped him short. "I didn't take it. Honest," Willie said. "Somebody's out to get me. I've been framed." And then, tough Willie Landers began to cry.

Dave and Sam were so embarrassed they didn't know where to look. Willie pulled out his white handkerchief and blew his nose. For the second time that day, the key fell out of it and onto the floor. And once again, Dave stooped to pick it up. But this time, Willie didn't stop him.

"You got in here with this key?" Dave asked.

Willie nodded.

"Okay, if you didn't take this money, then: One—What's it doing in your locker? Two—What did you put in your locker this afternoon? Three—What are you doing here tonight?"

Willie sniffled. "All right . . . I'll . . . tell."

Sam and Dave waited.

Willie began slowly, "Since my . . . uh . . . trouble last year, my parents, especially my old man, won't let me do anything, practically. I'm supposed to come home no later than four o'clock every day, and I have to be in bed by seven-thirty. And on top of that, my old man won't let me watch any TV or play any video games. . . . And, worst of all, he won't let me read comics . . ." He paused, and Sam and Dave could see tears welling up in his eyes again.

"Go on," Dave said once more, this time very gently.

"I . . . I have . . . had . . . this great collection of comics. My old man threw them out, but I saved 'em and moved 'em here. Then I made a copy of dad's key and started sneaking in here a couple of nights a week. My parents never check up on me once I'm in my room. See, they think I'm sleeping."

"Weren't you afraid of getting caught here?" Sam asked.

"Not really. I go into that supply closet." He pointed to a door. "There's a light inside and all. If I go in and close the door, nobody can tell I'm there.

Hey, how did you guys catch me?"

"We went to your house to talk with you and saw you sneaking out. Then, we followed you," said Sam.

"Willie, why did you say you *had* a great collection of comics?" Dave asked.

The tears started trickling down Willie's cheeks. "They're gone. All gone. You can see for yourself."

Sam and Dave peered inside his locker. It was empty.

Dave faced Willie. "How do we know you're telling the truth? Maybe you made the whole story up. Maybe there never were any comics and you just came here tonight to get this money you put in your locker today." Dave waved the wad at him.

"I'm not lying. I swear it. I don't know how the money got in here."

"Dave, look at this," Sam said. He'd reached up on the top shelf of the locker. In his hand was a single comic.

Dave took it from his brother. He looked at it. It was an old *Superman* comic. Then he looked at Willie. "How many comics did you have in this locker?"

"Seventeen or eighteen. A bunch of *Superman* and *Spiderman,* some *X-Men* and *Wonder Woman.* A few *Action Comics.* . . . Now do you believe me?"

"Let's say for now I do," Dave said. "But then we've got an even bigger mystery. Who took the money, ditched it here and swiped your comics. And why would somebody bother to take a bunch of old comics anyway?"

"Somebody's got it in for me," said Willie. "Somebody's trying to frame me."

"Who'd want to do that?" Dave asked, looking at Sam.

And at once, he knew they were thinking of the same person: Darryl Gaines.

6

Zzrroom! Darryl Gaines pitched a paper airplane through the air.

It hit Patti on the nose. She'd fashioned her own plane from a piece of paper she'd scooped off the floor near her locker and threw it at Darryl. It missed him and landed in Sam's hair.

The bell rang.

"Whoaaa!" Darryl and Patti said, racing off.

Sam picked the paper plane off his head and yawned.

"Wake up," Dave said, yawning himself.

They'd been up late going over the facts of

the case. Someone wanted to frame Willie. Some-one who hated him. Willie had stolen money from three kids last year: Laurie Peters, Jimmy Pappas and Darryl Gaines. Laurie was absent the day of the theft. Jimmy had moved away. That left Darryl. Sam and Dave decided to talk to him after school.

Willie arrived. "Did you find 'em?" he whispered eagerly.

"Not yet," Dave said.

"You didn't tell anybody about the money, did you?" he demanded, turning red. "Or about my . . . uh . . . being . . . uh . . . upset."

"No."

"Okay. . . . But you better do something. Soon."

The second bell rang.

"Come on. We're going to be late," Dave said.

Sam thought he heard his brother heave a sigh of relief.

Wondering what they were going to do about Willie and the money if they didn't find the culprit, Sam absentmindedly carried the plane to class. Ms. Corfein wasn't in yet. When he sat down, Sam noticed the plane in his hand. He admired the construction. Patti had done a good job. He began to unfold the plane to see just how she'd made it. And as he did, the writing on the paper caught his eye. It said:

Free Of Ugly Nasty Dogs Biting Under Your Excellent Roof Try Our New Improved Giant Hound Tenderizer Special Instructions X-mas To Use Right Tall Large Extra

"Huh?" he said. This doesn't make sense, he thought. It must be a joke. But he wondered why the joke was giving him goose bumps.

7

Sam carried his tray, on which he had a plate of chicken chow mein covered with soggy noodles and a container of milk, over to the table where Dave and Rita O'Toole were already sitting.

Dave greeted his brother by poking his chow mein. "How can you eat this stuff?" he said and took a bite from the liverwurst sandwich his mother had made him.

"I like it," Sam said simply. "And I don't like liverwurst."

Dave shrugged. Then he said, "Rita was just about to show me a substitution code, whatever that is."

Sam smiled. Rita knew a lot about codes and ciphers. She was always reading about them. Sam wondered if he'd ever be as smart as she was. He doubted it.

"Look." Rita opened her notebook and wrote down:

ZPV BSF JO EBOHFS.

"What do you think it says?" she asked.

"You got me."

"Wrong."

Dave threw a napkin at her.

Rita laughed. "Okay," she said, adjusting her glasses. "Substitute for each letter the letter that comes before it alphabetically. Now, try reading it."

"Y-O-U A-R-E I-N D-A-N-G-E-R. You are in danger. Hey, that's neat," Dave said.

"Another substitution code substitutes the letter that comes *after* each letter . . ."

With fingers just a little greasy from picking the noodles off the chow mein, Sam took the message he'd found out of his notebook. "How about this? Can you read it?" he asked. Rita and Dave stared at the words.

Suddenly a paper plane landed on top of the message.

Darryl retrieved it. "Sorry guys," he said. "How's the private eye biz these days?"

"Busy," Dave answered.

Darryl laughed and walked away.

"It'll take me a while to decipher this," Rita finally said.

"It's definitely a code?"

"It sure looks like one to me. Where'd you get it?"

Sam explained.

"Do you think Patti wrote it?"

"I don't know. It might be hers—or it might be someone else's. I only saw her pick the paper up off the floor. You think it's a clue?" Sam looked straight at his brother.

Dave felt the same funny feeling move through him that Sam had felt before. He nodded at Sam. "Something tells me it might be."

Sam slowly nodded back.

8

"Ugly Nasty Dogs . .*. New Improved Giant Hound Tenderizer . . ." This is really crazy, Rita thought, studying the message. Sam had given it to her to decode. The bus she was riding hit a bump and she fell against Roger Blitzman, sitting next to her. "Sorry," she said.

"Th-that's all r-right," he stuttered.

She stared at the note again.

"Look at this one. Isn't that hairstyle ridiculous!" Patti Terroni's voice shrieked behind her.

"Ten bucks worth of ridiculous," Mona Green said.

"Wow! You mean between this and the other magazine, I'll get thirty-five dollars!"

"Minus seven bucks."

"Huh? How come?"

"That's my commission."

"Commission! Geez, you sound like . . . like my father."

Rita sighed. They're so distracting, she thought, trying to focus on the code in front of her. "Special Instructions X-mas . . ."

The bus stopped. Roger excused himself, stepped over Rita's feet and got off.

"Well, if you want to be like that, let's write out a contract," Patti said.

"Honestly!" Mona said.

"Darn, I can't find my pen that writes green. You have it?"

"No, I gave it back to you."

Patti leaned over the seat. "Rita." She tapped her on the shoulder. "Rita, do you have a pen?"

Rita turned her head and saw both Patti and Mona looking at her. She put her hand over the note. "I'm using it," she said.

"Oh, never mind. I'll use this pencil. It's legal in pencil, isn't it?"

Rita shook her head. They're unbelievable, she

thought. She slowly took her hand away from the note and stared once again at the strange message. It was then that something else about it struck her. It was written in green ink.

9

The interview with Darryl wasn't going well. Sam and Dave couldn't let on that they'd found the money, so they had to use the indirect approach.

"Heard you got a good collection of comics. I'd love to see them sometime. I'm a comics fan myself," Dave said, as he walked alongside Darryl.

Darryl just stared at him blankly. "Comics? I don't have any comics. Who told you I did?"

"Oh, somebody. I forget who. . . . Maybe it was Willie Landers."

"Willie Landers! Even if I had a comics collection, I wouldn't have told him about it. He'd probably steal it."

For once, Dave didn't know what to say.

"Since when are you friendly with Willie Landers?" demanded Darryl.

Dave regained his cool. He looked Darryl straight in the eye. "Willie has his good points."

"Yeah? The only good point I've seen of his is the top of his head." Darryl walked away.

"Well, he didn't seem to know anything about the comics. But, unlike Willie, he *is* a good actor," Dave said, remembering Darryl's performance in last year's talent show.

Sam frowned. "There's something we're not seeing," he said.

"What?"

"I'm not sure. But I'll know it when I see it."

Dave groaned at the joke.

10

Rita got off the bus and walked slowly toward home. She was still staring at the note. The sun was already going down and Rita idly thought, Ms. Corfein sure did keep us in a long time. She rounded a corner. This code is either so complicated or so simple I can't figure it out. "Free of Ugly Nasty Dogs Biting . . ." Suddenly, she let out a yelp and then a cough. "Help, I can't see! I can't see!" she yelled, coughing and choking as a cloud of something white and dusty got into her eyes and nose. Someone grabbed her hand, then gave her a shove. She tripped

and skinned her knee. *"Owww!"* she cried out. But her eyes were beginning to clear. She wiped them and looked around. No one was there. She didn't know which way the attacker had come from and she decided it was too late to run after him or her anyway. She stared down at her hands. They were covered with powder. Baby powder, from the smell of it. She scrambled to her feet. Her knee was bleeding a little and it stung, but the cut wasn't very serious. Someone couldn't have really wanted to hurt her, but then why . . . and who. . . . Thoughts clanged in her head. She adjusted her backpack, which had gone askew when she fell, and picked up some change that had fallen out of her pocket. Have I got everything? No, something's missing. Something . . . oh no, the message. It's gone. Someone took it. Someone who threw powder at me and knocked me down. That message must be important after all, Rita said to herself. I'd better tell Sam and Dave. Immediately.

11

Sam and Dave were explaining to their mother why they were late when the phone rang. Ms. Bean picked it up. "Hello . . . just a minute." She held out the phone. "It's Rita."

While Sam screwed up his courage to take the phone from his mother, Dave took it. "Hi, Rita. Did you decode the note yet? What? What? Holy smoke! You got what? Could you tell who it was?" Green ink? Patti Terroni's pen?"

Sam leaped to his feet. "Did something happen to her? Is she . . ."

"*Shhh,*" Dave said. "Here. She wants to talk to you."

Sam was so upset he forgot to be shy. "What happened? Are you okay?" he nearly shouted into the phone.

"Someone knocked me down. I feel fine, but the note is gone," Rita answered, sounding quite calm.

"*Wow!*"

"Yes. . . . Listen, Sam. Was that note the original?"

"Yeah," he answered.

"Okay, then, did you memorize it?"

If Rita could have seen him, she would've noticed that Sam was blushing. He had a remarkable ability to memorize almost anything—although he didn't necessarily understand what he was memorizing. He was a little embarrassed by this talent—probably because when he was younger his teachers often made him recite long speeches which bored the other students and made them sort of annoyed at Sam, even though he would just as soon have hidden in the boys' room than stood up there in front of the class. "Yeah," he said once again to Rita.

"Great! Recite it to me and I'll write it down."

"Okay," Sam said, and did.

When he hung up, he turned to Dave. "Wow," he said again.

"Yeah. She doesn't know if it was a guy or a girl who knocked her down. She didn't see the person."

"What did she tell you about Patti Terroni's pen?"

"It had green ink—and so did the note. Plus it was missing."

"If it was missing, anyone could have used it. Or maybe someone else has a green pen; they're not uncommon."

"I know." Dave sighed. "That's the problem with this case—too many people could have written that note; too many people could have taken the money and the comics. And maybe the note has nothing to do with the money."

"Then why would someone have swiped it from Rita?"

"Hmmm."

Then Sam said, "Dave, who knew that Rita had the note?"

"That's a good question. Mona and Patti, probably. Darryl Gaines, maybe. His paper plane landed right on top of it."

"Darryl Gaines. Again." Sam sighed.

"Yeah, again," said Dave.

12

"What time is it?" Dave asked.

"Five-thirty. Dinner'll be ready soon," Sam said.

Dave drummed his fingers on the headboard of his bed. "It must be a hard code," he said. "She's taking a long time."

"Dave, let's go over the case once more."

"Okay. Crime: class money stolen. Suspects: Willie Landers, Patti Terroni because she was in the classroom at lunchtime, and everybody else in the school. Money shows up in Willie Landers's locker. He claims comics stolen. Motive: framing Willie. Suspect: Darryl Gaines. His locker is even near Willie's. He could have easily learned Willie's combination."

"But how could Darryl have gotten into Ms. Corfein's locker?" Sam asked.

"Hmmm . . . we keep coming back to that one," said Dave.

"Patti's good friends with Darryl. Maybe she decided to frame Willie for Darryl's sake."

"How could *she* have gotten into Ms. Corfein's locker? Maybe Willie did it after all. Maybe the comics are just a lie."

"No, I think Willie was telling the truth," Sam said firmly.

"Ms. Corfein's locker, Ms. Corfein's locker . . . Roger put the money in . . . then . . . wait . . . could it be . . . holy smoke!" yelled Dave.

Then, the doorbell rang.

Sam and Dave tensed. They heard their mother open the door and say, "Well, hi, Rita. Did you bike over here? The boys are upstairs. We'll be having dinner soon. Want to stay?"

"Maybe, Ms. Bean," they heard Rita answer. "I've got to talk to Sam and Dave first." In another moment, she was in their room. "I've decoded it!" She grinned triumphantly. "I would've done it on the bus if that silly Patti Terroni and Mona Green hadn't been going on behind me about old movie magazines and how much they're worth."

"Never mind. What does it say?" Sam and Dave said simultaneously.

Rita produced a copy of the original message:

Free Of Ugly Nasty Dogs Biting Under Your Excellent Roof Try Our New Improved Giant Hound Tenderizer Special Instructions X-mas To Use Right Tall Large Extra

"It's so simple it's embarrassing. Here." She

deftly circled the first letter of each word, so the message now looked like this:

(F)ree (O)f (U)gly (N)asty (D)ogs (B)iting (U)nder (Y)our (E)xcellent (R)oof (T)ry (O)ur (N)ew (I)mproved (G)iant (H)ound (T)enderizer (S)pecial (I)nstructions (X)-mas (T)o (U)se (R)ight (T)all (L)arge (E)xtra

"Now read the circled letters."

"F-O-U-N-D . . ." began Sam.

But Dave interrupted, " 'Found Buyer Tonight Six Turtle.' Rita, you're a genius!"

Rita beamed. Then she said, "Well, that's the message all right, but what does it mean?"

"I think I know," Sam said slowly.

"Me too," said Dave. "And we better hurry up. It's five–fifty-five!"

"Where are you going? Dinner's ready," Sam and Dave's mother called as they grabbed their jackets from the hall closet.

"Don't worry, Mom. This won't take too long," Dave said.

He, Sam and Rita raced out the door. As usual, Sam was in the lead, with Rita, who still didn't know where they were heading, following close behind and Dave last. They ran down the familiar streets until they came to the playground. Then Sam slowed down. The others did too.

Standing by the stone turtle were two figures. The streetlight shining on them revealed a middle-aged man with a bald head and a girl about their age.

"Mona Green!" Rita gasped.

Fortunately, neither Mona nor the man heard. "So, where is this friend of yours?" he was saying impatiently. "It's cold out here and I haven't got all evening. Why the heck did he insist we meet in this playground anyway?"

"He's kind of . . . uh . . . secretive," Mona said. "But very reliable. Don't worry, he'll be here any minute."

Just then, a short figure came into view. He had a hat pulled down over his eyes and a scarf wrapped around the lower half of his face. Silently, he handed a fat envelope to the man.

The man opened it and took out a stack of comics. "My heavens, these are beauties!"

It was at that moment that Dave, striding forward, said, "They're also hot."

"What? Who are you?"

"I'm Dave Bean. This is my brother Sam and our friend Rita O'Toole. And those comics you've got were stolen from Willie Landers."

"Stolen!" The man turned to Mona. "What do you know about this?" he demanded.

"Nothing . . . I . . ." she turned helplessly to the figure in the hat and scarf.

The short figure seemed to deflate. He let out a sigh. Slowly, he took off the hat. "I'm glad this is over. . . . Yes, you're right. The comics are Willie's. I never meant to steal them. Or the class money either. It's just . . . my father's out of work, and my mother's having another baby. I saw the money and . . . something happened to me. I remembered this mystery I read and I put the money in my pocket. Then, I got scared . . ." Slowly, he began to unwind the scarf. "I thought they were going to search me. I wanted to ditch the money. I went down the row of lockers, rattling them. One was open. I was going to throw the money in when I saw these comics. You see, I know about comics. I knew these were worth a lot. So I took them—including the one in the envelope which I put the money into. I didn't know whose comics they were. I didn't want to know. Mona sent me the note—but she's innocent. She didn't know the comics were stolen. When I saw that Rita had somehow got hold of the note, I threw baby powder at her (I bought it when I got off the bus) and got the note away. I'm sorry if I scared you, Rita. And I'm glad you caught me." The scarf slid from his face.

Rita gasped for the second time that evening. The boy standing in front of her was the last person in the world she expected to hear that confession from. He was Roger Blitzman.

13

"Ms. Corfein, I was looking in my jeans yesterday and I found this," Roger said, handing her a wad of bills. "I must've been thinking about something else when I stuck the money in my pocket. I feel really stupid."

Sam and Dave, standing right outside the door, smiled at each other. Roger was making his speech just the way they'd told him to.

"My goodness, all that trouble and the money was safe all along," said Ms. Corfein.

"Well, not exactly . . ." Roger began.

"What do you mean?" she asked sharply.

"Uh-oh," whispered Dave.

"I . . . I mean . . . uh . . . my mom could've washed my pants."

Sam clapped his hand over his mouth so no one would hear him laugh.

"Well, it's safe now, anyway. And anyone can make a mistake, so don't feel too bad, Roger. I'll tell Mr. Bryant to announce that the money was found and there'll be nothing more said about it."

"Thank you, Ms. Corfein," said Roger. "I think

I'll hang up my coat now." He walked outside.

"Congratulations," Dave said.

"I . . . I still feel bad. That wasn't right, to lie. I'm still a thief."

"You didn't lie," said Sam. "You *were* thinking about something else when you put the money in your pocket instead of in Ms. Corfein's locker. And Ms. Corfein's right, anyone can make a mistake."

Roger smiled at him.

"One thing I still don't get is why Mona sent you that note. Why didn't she just call you and tell you she had a buyer?"

Roger smiled again. "It's a game we have. We've been writing notes in code to each other since third grade. I sent her a note first, telling her I got hold of some rare comics. She knows a lot about old comics and magazines, too, and she found a buyer fast because she'd sold him stuff before."

"I didn't even know you and Mona were friends," Dave said. "I never saw you together in school."

"Mona's been too busy with her magazine business," Roger said, a little sadly.

After a pause, Sam said, "I hope your dad finds another job."

Roger's face brightened. "He did. He told me last night when I got home from the playground."

"Then, everything's worked out just fine," said Dave.

"Almost," added Sam, looking over Dave's shoulder.

He turned and saw Willie Landers stomping toward them.

"Well, Bean Brothers, Private Eyes. Where are my comics?"

"Right here," Dave said smoothly, producing them.

Willie grabbed them and leafed through the stack. "Hey, they're all here. Er . . . thanks." They could tell he wasn't used to saying that. Then his face got a suspicious look. "Where'd you find them?"

"I took them," Roger said boldly.

"You what?" Willie clenched his fists.

"I . . . I . . . I know someone who'll give you fifteen hundred for them."

"Fifteen hundred what?"

"Dollars."

Willie looked like someone had hit him right between the eyes. "You're kidding?"

"No. Do you know what a *Superman* comic, issue number twenty-five in good condition, is worth? Well, I'll explain." He and Willie walked off together toward their lockers.

Willie's voice echoed down the hall, "Blitzman, you're a man after my own heart."

Sam and Dave looked at each other and began to laugh.

About the Author

Marilyn Singer is the author of three other Sam and Dave Mystery Stories, THE CASE OF THE SABOTAGED SCHOOL PLAY, LEROY IS MISSING, and THE CASE OF THE CACKLING CAR; several novels, including IT CAN'T HURT FOREVER, THE COURSE OF TRUE LOVE NEVER DID RUN SMOOTH, THE FIDO FRAMEUP (a mystery) and NO APPLAUSE, PLEASE; as well as a number of picture books. She is a mystery fan, proud of having read the complete works of Agatha Christie, Dorothy Sayers and other notable writers.

Ms. Singer lives with her husband, three dogs, several cats, pigeons and a parakeet in a Brooklyn brownstone.

About the Illustrator

Judy Glasser's terrific pictures have appeared in THE CASE OF THE SABOTAGED SCHOOL PLAY, LEROY IS MISSING, and THE CASE OF THE CACKLING CAR, as well as in THE PROBLEM WITH PULCIFER (Florence Parry Heide), MR. RADAGAST MAKES AN UNEXPECTED JOURNEY (Sharon Nastik), and several other children's books and publications including *The New York Times* and *Esquire.* Her work has also appeared in shows at the Art Directors Club and the Society of Illustrators. Ms. Glasser lives in New York City.